# Date Nights in Rogue Stone

## Rogue Stone After Dark, Volume 2

McKayla Jade

Published by McKayla Jade, 2024.

This is a work of fiction. Similarities to real people, places, or events are entirely coincidental.

DATE NIGHTS IN ROGUE STONE

**First edition. April 12, 2024.**

Copyright © 2024 McKayla Jade.

ISBN: 979-8224500598

Written by McKayla Jade.

If you've read the first book in this series, you know what to expect here, however, I went a bit darker on some of these stories. The very last is way out of the realm of Rogue Stone, BUT this book is only based on that world. So, adapt and adjust as you need. These stories are meant to give you and your partner or partners ideas for fun. If you enjoyed this one, hold on to your panties. There will be a third coming soon.

McKayla

# Date Night #11 Dancing

Cassidy's laughter rang through the hall. Hawk could not hide his smile as he spun her around in front of him. Nicole was trying to teach them a new dance and Cassidy was stumbling more than she was dancing. She just could not seem to get in time with the steps. He pulled her close and held her to his chest as he counted them in and he told her. "Follow my lead. Just this once, follow me." He grinned as they stepped and she frowned.

"I do follow you." She stumbled again.

He stopped. "Would you like to try that again?"

Cassidy huffed. "Well most of the time I follow you."

"He's right Cassidy." Nicole stepped up to them. "If you would let him lead, all you have to do is follow and your steps will fall right in behind his."

Cassidy glared at Nicole but kept her mouth shut. She knew better than to lash out with her words. Her temper was fierce and it had wounded many in the past. She took a deep breath and nodded. Hawk twirled her once more and they were off again. "One two three," He chanted and the outside world fell away. His voice wrapped around her and she melted into him like butter. She followed his voice as though she were in a trance. "One two three and spin."

She stumbled a couple more times and each time he caught her and started back over until she was flowing like water across the floor.

They kept going and the other two couples finally moved closer and all were dancing to the music when he turned Cassidy back into his arms one last time. Before the momentum was gone and before she could realize what he was about, he picked her up and carried her up the stairs to their chambers on the top floor. He had already requested the room to be readied.

Upon opening the door he was pleasantly surprised by the care taken in their chambers. The fire burned low, casting out the draft of the early winter cold. The bed sheets had been turned down and the room was lit in a soft glow of candlelight.

Cassidy gasped. "Hawk, did you?"

Her unfinished sentence confirmed he had done well. Cassidy had been very busy lately and had taken little to no time to rest. This would be her night to do just that. He took her hand and turned her back to him again and this time pulled her into his chest. When she looked up he took possession of her lips. She pushed back with a boldness he had not felt from her in a long time. Her arms came up to wrap around his neck and she raised herself up on the tips of her toes. Her murmured nonsense and little moans drove him onward. He growled as he lifted her off the floor and carried her to the settee near the fireplace. The room was warm but a draft here or there added a little thrill to playing naked.

"Mmm" She murmured as he set her down and pulled away to shed himself of his clothes. "Come back down here." She whispered as he was unfastening his shirt. He bent over and she took over with her nimble fingers. She went about her work so fast he barely noticed his waist band loosen before he shed his shirt. Her hand came up to slide over his muscled chest and over his shoulders. With one hand on the back of the settee, and one hand on the side of her face, he whispered. "Little One, let me shed these clothes and then we can play freely."

The blush that crept over her face after all these years still made him hard. He would never get tired of seeing her shyness. She knew him as he knew her and still she was shy about seeing him undress. He shook his head. His woman suited him as none other could.

Hawk undressed in front of her and even her ears felt warm. Why was she like this? She had seen him dress and undress thousands of times. *'Perhaps this time, it is because I intend to ravish you'* He broke into her thoughts to tease her and she could not stop the grin from splitting her face.

She reached for him. "I adore you." She whispered.

"Good." He whispered back before kissing her.

"Good?" What an odd thing.

"Yes. I would not want you to adore anyone else and if you adore me you will look to no one else." Hawk was smug. She was his and always would be. He kissed her, effectively silencing her.

She let him. She had no more words to say. She wanted him. Needed him. He adjusted himself over her and continued his warm kisses from her lips to her cheek, down her neck and lower still. She gasped. He glanced up for a moment but kept going. She leaned her head back as he took a nipple into his mouth and suckled. She brought her hands up his sides, over his tight muscles there and arched herself upward to accommodate him.

Hawk moved to her other breast and repeated the play and just as she thought she would burst, he slid a finger into her. First one, gentle and easy and slow. "Hmmm." She moaned and closed her eyes as the delicious feelings swamped her. "Hawk."

He didn't look up at her, he did not need to. "Little One, take a deep breath. You have to wait."

Her heart raced and she panted. He could not be serious. He wasn't going to let her have release. She tried for a deep breath and it came out more like a gasp. She raised up and kissed his chest where he hovered above her. She licked and kissed and ran her fingers through the light dusting of hair there. Slowly, as though she did not mean to do so, she slid her hands down his stomach and side right down to his hips. Slowly, her fingers barely touching his skin, she slid them down to cup his bollocks. She ducked her head when he growled. She loved pleasing him and if she was not allowed to have a release, she would torment him until he forgot his command.

Slowly, finger by finger she wrapped her hand around his velvet steel shaft. Hesitating for the mereest of moments she began sliding her hand up and down the length of him. A few strokes and he was thrusting his hips, driving himself forward, through her fingers, the tip touching her belly. She giggled when she realized his eyes were closed and his jaw was clenched tight.

"Struggling?" She asked.

"No more than ye." He growled and leaned his head low to kiss her lightly on her lips. "But if I allow you to continue, I will spend myself in your hands."

"Oh dear. We must not have that." She was relentless in her teasing. She stroked him faster.

He reached for her hand and removed it from him before he nudged her legs apart with his knee, and sent his velvet steel inside her. She arched her back and moaned as pleasure coursed through her, lighting every nerve on fire. The rush of energy made her gasp and Hawk increased his pace, giving her no time to breathe. She wrapped her arms around his shoulders and held on as best she could. Gods he was good at this.

Her heart was racing and she was uncertain if it would ever slow it down. The glimpses she was able to catch of his muscles straining and bunching above her made her lick her lips. She was still just as hungry for him as when they had started. She lifted her head to kiss his chest again. She licked and nipped and kissed him there. The low growl rumbling deep inside him drove her onward as his cock slid in and out of her. Her racing heart had her licking her lips and trying to catch her breath but all she could manage were short gasps between his withdrawal and his cock sliding deep inside her.

"Cassidy, fly with me." The command was given between his clenched teeth and she closed her eyes just before stars exploded in her vision. He thrust once more and she floated within the clouds. Hawk's big body rested on top of hers, but he was careful to keep most of his weight on his arms, so as not to hurt her. She slid her hands up and down his broad muscular back, enjoying the feeling of his muscles bunching and twitching beneath them.

He huffed out a breath, raised up and kissed her forehead and then her lips. "Gods, little one, the things I feel when we make love are nothing less than astounding." He wrapped his arms around her and rolled onto his back, taking her with him.

She kissed his chest. "I love ye." She whispered.

"For always and forever, Little One." he whispered back.

MODERN DAY ADAPTATION ~~ Take dance classes. If you already know how to dance, learn a new dance. So, not much modification needed here.

# Date Night #12 Volunteering

Gareth growled as she got further away. Damn woman.

"Megan. Hold. I will come with you, but let me get some supplies first." He turned back to the sheds near the stable. He gathered some rope and a couple shovels and with a shake of his head, turned back to Megan. His damned woman was grinning from ear to ear and had clasped her hands in front of her.

"Don't. Don't do it." Before the words had even left his lips, Megan let out a squeal so loud most of the courtyard turned in their direction. Gareth sighed and started walking along the path that would lead to the farmers place.

"Thank you, Gareth." Megan whispered. "I know you don't share my enthusiasm, but it will greatly help Mr. Mcfarland and his wife who is a dear friend."

He reached over and took her hand in his as they walked. He brought it to his lips and kissed her knuckles. "Megan, I truly do not mind helping. I was but hoping I could help myself to the loving of my wife this day."

The blush that crept up her neck all the way to her hairline told him he had hit his target. "We have had little time lately to be alone, with the children and the demands of Rogue Stone pressing down upon us." He confessed. "I just wanted an afternoon alone with my wife." He raised her hand and kissed her knuckles again. "However if Macfarland needs help, we must help. It is who we are."

"I am sorry, love. You can have me later."she whispered.

Gareth had to pick his jaw up off his chest. Megan never spoke so boldly. Lest not out in the open. It was his turn to stand there immobilized and watch after his wife, slowly walking away as if she were not swinging her hips just so and as though she had not thrown a teasing glance over her shoulder. He shook his head and set off after her. In just a few steps he was right beside her and all too soon they crested the hill overlooking the farm and sure as he breathed air, that cow was well and truly stuck to its shoulders in the thick mud. Gareth sighed. This was going to be a long day.

As he started down the hill ahead of Megan he called to her. "Ye will owe me big on this one."

The blush of her cheeks he'd caught when he glanced back at her made him smile. The view ahead of him however, wiped it from his face. As he approached, the farmer called out to him.

"Thank ye, sir. Me and the boys have been tryin' all morning to get her outta there. Stubborn cow won't move."

"There might be an easier way." Gareth hoped he wasn't just blowing smoke. As he got closer he let his wings burst forth. He stretched them wide and high, hoping to scare the damned cow out of the mud, but rather than run and pull herself out of the thick quagmire, her eyes went wide and she let out a loud mooing sound, just before she collapsed.

"Gareth." Megan screeched. "You've killed her."

"I've done nothing of the sort." He bluffed, hoping it wasn't true, but if it were they would have steaks for the evening meal.

The little calf on the bank cried out and ran back and forth continuing to call for his momma. Shockingly the damned cow shook her head and started trying once again to get herself out of the mud.

"Megan toss me that rope." Gareth told her. "I'll at least be able to get that on her neck easy enough, if I fly over her."

"Could you just pick her up?" Megan asked him.

"I would if I could, but she weighs a bit too much for that and the mud will add weight."

Megan chewed on her fingernail and waited to see what else she could do to help the men get that poor cow out of the mud. Gareth was hovering just above the frightened thing, but she kept thrashing about, making it difficult for him to slip the loop over her head.

With the rope finally in place, Gareth tugged on it to get a firm grasp and handed the first link of it to McFarland. "Here. You hold this tight and I'll help you pull."

"I don't know Gareth, I don't want to hurt her."

"We won't if she's got a lick of sense, she'll come toward us, so as soon as she does, get outta her way."

A few tugs on the rope later and a few choice words, Gareth was starting to doubt himself.

"Maybe." Megan's small voice came from just behind him and he glanced over his shoulder. "Maybe I can help. Ease up on the rope for a second?"

He took a deep sigh of relief. He could use a break and so could McFarland, but his breath caught in his throat when Megan started taking off her shoes.

"What are ye doing?" He asked.

"I have an idea." She raised her hand and showed him she held a fist full of red clover. "She loves these and her pasture is barren of them."

Gareth shook his head. "And I suppose you are going to lure her out with a treat."

"We tried that." Mcfarland protested while still holding tight to the rope. "The damned thing wouldn't budge."

Gareth glared at him. Megan was a Lady. He did not need to use such language around her and Mcfarland bowed. "Sorry, sir. Megan, lass, we've tried everything but pulling her out."

Megan smiled. "Maybe so, but you most certainly have not tried sweet talking her." The blush on Megan's face was as deep red as he'd ever seen it. "Every girl likes to be sweet-talked."

He opened his mouth to reprimand her and closed it just as fast. The courage it took her to banter so, cost her a lot. There was no need for him to publicly shame her.

"Gareth, watch..." Before McFarland could say more, Gareth caught only a blur of brown fur and horns before he was knocked into the mud.

The cow pushed her way past Gareth straight toward Megan. She sucked in a breath, worried about Gareth, who was now in the direct path of a hungry cow. Megan dropped the clover and tried to run before the cow pushed her over too. She also didn't make it very far before Mcfarland picked her up and spun in a circle to toss her into the grass on his far side, out of the way of the charging cow. She hit the ground hard and coughed before turning to get a look at Gareth. The mud covering his face made him look even more intimidating than he had before. Megan sucked in a wild breath and stood up on shaky legs. She had not realized the cow had scared her so much.

"Megan. Come here." Gareth commanded and she was helpless to do more than walk toward him.

"Megan. It is all right. You are not hurt are you?" He asked and she saw Mcfarland out of the corner of her eye paused in his tracks.

She shook her head before she answered. "No. I am not hurt. I was just scared, but I am all right. I am just fine." She could not help repeating herself. She was shaky just now and if she stuttered, they would just have to forgive her.

Gareth came toward her, bent his face to hers and kissed her gently. "Megan. It is all right. You are safe with me."

Gareth whispered words soothed her like nothing else could. They always had. She was not sure if it was the timbre of his voice or the particular words he used, but whatever it was, she loved it.

Gareth wrapped her in his arms and before she had taken a full breath they were high up in the air. He did not slow down until they reached the private lake on the top of the mountain, above the waterfall most folks enjoyed. This spot, however, was reserved for the warriors alone and he had sent out the call for privacy here. Megan sighed as he set her down on the grass near the water. She moved close to the bank and started washing off her feet.

"We've forgotten my shoes." She murmured.

Gareth sat down next to her and wrapped one arm around her shoulders to tell her. "Your shoes were the last thing on my mind. Getting you in this water seemed more important."

"Gareth it's still too early in the year for that. This water is too chilly to play in." She protested and he grinned before he took possession of her lips. While he had her distracted, he snapped his fingers and glanced toward the now steaming water. Her gasp told him she had not been all that distracted.

"Gareth." One word. Just his name on her lips and he was as hard as a rock. He turned back to her, not bothering to answer her question, but kissed her again. His hand slid up her side and his thumb grazed the underside of her breast. He pulled his head back to kiss her cheek, then her jaw, down her neck to her shoulder. As he went he stripped her of her clothing and her hands followed his lead. Her nimble fingers worked the buckles and ties of his trousers. His boots, like her shoes, were long forgotten back at McFarland's farm.

He pulled back from her just as she got his belt unbuckled. He made short work of their clothing and tossed it haphazardly in a pile, before picking her up. She did not say a word. Her cheeks were so red he was sure they felt like fire. He kissed her once more, and laid her against the soft moss and grass lining the bank of the stream. He positioned himself over her and trailed kisses down to her belly and back up to her lips. His fingers messaged and caressed her inner thighs. She whimpered and moaned and he could hold no longer. He took himself in hand and lined himself up with her warm velvet folds. She cried out as he entered her tight sheath and slid all the way to the hilt. He paused as he always did and until she looked at him he would not give her what her body craved.

Her eyes opened and he pulled almost all the way out and slid back in half way making her gasp. He finally gave her what her body was begging for and slid his hard cock in and out slowly, methodically, then a bit faster and she whimpered one word. "*More*" and he was lost. He pumped his hips forward and back thrusting his cock deep. Then faster and faster until he threw his own body down over her. He held himself above her and continued his rhythmic strokes until she gasped his name.

"There." She gasped and he pumped harder.

"Yes." she whimpered and he grunted as he thrust one last time and his own body burst from the inside out.

"That's my girl." He whispered as his body pulsed and his cock throbbed one last time, completely spent.

They spent what felt like an hour laying in each other's arms before he picked her up and carried her toward the stream and small pool.

As he reached the shoreline she held tighter and he glanced down to reassure her. Her eyes were tightly shut and her brow furrowed. He stopped in his tracks and laughed out loud.

"Megan, open your eyes." He told her. "I warmed the water, that is why it was steaming a moment ago."

"You did? I thought you did." She stammered. "I wasn't sure."

He walked out into the water and as he moved further into the warmed water, Megan held tighter and if he wasn't mistaken, she was lifting her rear up as much as she could and still be in his arms. He lowered his head and took a nipple between his teeth. She sighed and relaxed. He licked and sucked before he took another step, which sent both of them deeper. The water lapped around her arse and belly where they hung lower down in his arms. He bent his knees to lower them both and she sighed against his lips.

Megan put one hand to the side of his face and whispered, with her eyes still closed. "This is so very good."

Gareth chuckled and bent to kiss her forehead. "I wonder though, is it so good, you no longer need your husband?"

Her eyes popped open. "Oh gods no. That isn't how I meant it." She was quick to amend.

He silenced her with a kiss and told her. "I was only jesting."

He took a nipple into his mouth once again and rolled it between his teeth and tugged a bit. She moaned and laid her head back in the water. Her hair floated all around them and he held her. Letting their bodies relax. He kissed her neck, and leaned back against the bolder behind him to relax his own body.

MODERN DAY ADAPTATION~~ Find somewhere to volunteer or a neighbor that could use a hand and reward each other with a good time afterward, wherever you choose.

# Date Night # 13 Scavenger Hunt

Nicole bent to pick up the tiny piece of paper lying on the floor of her bedroom. Dalton had left earlier when summoned by the king. She didn't mind him leaving every once in a while, but sometimes like today, she felt just a little bit left out. Maybe she would join Cassidy and the other women who trained for battle and join her man one day. She unfolded the paper, making it twice the size it had seemed.

'*The path of most resistance has the most reward.*' She narrowed her gaze. That was the opposite of how she'd always heard it. Shouldn't she take the path of least resistance? She crossed the room and pulled open the door, intending to take the note to someone else. Maybe someone could tell her what it meant. She glanced up and there to her left the hallway was blocked by ropes. She stepped up to it and examined it. It wasn't magic of any sort. It seemed to be plain ordinary rope stretched across the hall several times. She glanced down at the folded paper in her hand.

She shrugged her shoulders and ducked through and stepped over the ropes. Once on the other side she followed the hall. Maybe there was something to the note she'd found. A few steps more and the hall got darker. She stopped and looked back the way she had come. Maybe she should go back. She shook her head. No, she would follow this. Maybe it would lead somewhere fun.

Just ahead was another scrap of paper. This one read, *'Find the faded rose and turn right, but don't forget to smell the roses along the way.'*

Odd. Why would she smell a wilted rose and there were not usually roses in this hallway. It simply led to the parapets. Most of the warriors used them to watch the walls and take off flying. She stopped when she came to a single rose laying on the floor. It had been there for sometime, for when she picked it up the head bent and one petal fell to the floor at her feet. When she stood back up she thought she saw a dark shadow disappear around the next corner. She hurried to follow and when she turned the corner an empty hall greeted her. She stood for a moment, just watching for movement. Then a little white piece of paper fluttered in wind she could not feel.

She shivered, rubbed her arms, and stepped toward it. Her heart was racing so fast now, she was certain if she stopped to listen, it could be heard throughout the hall. She unfolded it and read it. *'In the shadows awaits your prize, but are you brave enough?'* A chill rippled through her and she clenched her jaw. She wasn't sure if she was afraid, nervous, or excited. She took a deep breath in and a roar or kind of a roar, like that of a big cat filled the hallway. Her heart leapt up in her throat and nervous energy filled her. Her wings burst from her back and shoved her into the middle of the hallway.

"Shit." She crouched low and started to plan her next move when Dalton's laughter filled the air. She slowly stood back up but kept her back to the wall.

"Dalton?" She asked out loud. "Are you here?"

"Come further down the hall. I promise you are safe."

Completely caught off guard and unsure of her next steps, she sucked in a wild breath and forced herself to move forward.

"Calm yourself, Dearheart. I would never put you in danger."

"I thought I knew that, but I'm starting to wonder." She quipped. Against her own better judgment, she moved further down the dark hall and as she got to the corner, she pulled her sword and tucked her wings tight.

Just before she dared to peek around the corner, the big cat let out a call again. What in the world was that? Her curiosity won out and sword held at the ready as she stepped around the last corner. There was Dalton standing next to the most gorgeous little spotted cat she had ever laid eyes on.

She dropped to her knees and the white and black fur covered thing came right to her and tried again to make a roar. "A baby snow leopard? Dalton? That's why the roar sounded so odd."

Dalton leaned lazily against the wall and grinned. "It was orphaned in the mountains, but the rest of the story is classified."

She glanced up, but he clearly wasn't going to divulge any more information.

"Suffice it to say, he needed a home and you wanted a pet."

She reached out one hand to pet the beautiful thing and Dalton moved like lightning to get behind her. She hesitated until she got a look at the grin on his face. "Dalton, what are you up to?"

He leaned low, kissed her shoulder and whispered. "I gave you a kitty. Now I want your pussy on my cock."

Her whole body flushed hot. "Right here?"

"Right now." He told her. "I don't care where."

She licked her lips and asked once again. "The cat is really mine?"

"Forever." He kissed her cheek and wrapped his arms around her from behind. "Which is exactly how long it's been since I've held my mate in my arms. Now, let's go."

She started to hesitate, and he whispered before nipping her ear lobe. "It will follow. It knows you."

She couldn't argue with him nor did she want to. They made it no further than a random empty bedchamber. Dalton wrapped her in his arms and spun on his heel so as not to land on top of her as they fell on the bed. She squealed and the kitten cried from the doorway. She paid it no mind, but he summoned it and raised up to close the chamber door.

"Where..." Nicole didn't finish her sentence when she looked up. There was no need. He closed the door and turned back to her. He grinned and before she could guess his intent he leapt to the bed and braced himself to land on top of her. She laughed and kissed his upper arm when he came down over her. He held her head in his hands and leaned low to kiss her.

She closed her eyes and let the sensations overtake her. Dalton's hands slid down her sides, his thumbs grazing the side of her breast. The warmth of his hands seeped into her, and she purred. Somehow her clothes disappeared and so had his, but she didn't care just now. Her core throbbed for him and she arched her back pressing herself closer to him. She needed what only he could give her. He lifted his hips, pulling away, teasing her. Just as she opened her mouth to protest the head of his thick cock pressed at her core.

"Mmm-hmmm." She bit her lip as sensations swept her and the effort it took to open her eyes became too much. She arch to him as he slid inside her, stretching her, filling her. Slowly, in all the way, then a slow burn out. She could not keep quiet. Anyone might happen upon them. She bit her lip, but when he thrusted back into her, she let out a whimper. She glanced up at him and the grin on his face told her he was just getting started. "Dalton." His name a mere whisper across her swollen lips. Lips swollen from his kisses. She slid her hands up to cover her breast and roll each nipple between a thumb and finger. She tilted her head back and moaned while Dalton thrust his hips a bit faster now, and just a bit harder. She licked her lips and flashed him a smile before she wrapped her hands around his arms to pull herself up and kiss his chest, then his neck. She lowered herself back to the bed and lifted her hips to meet him and struggled to keep herself quiet, lest they should be caught.

He bent low over her and whispered. "Let go, let your body sing."

She took a deep breath and followed his command. A deep flush of euphoria swept her and filled her every pore. The wave was so intense she cried out and held tight as wave after wave crashed through her. "Dalton." She whispered.

He kissed her and took her last cry of release before he wrapped her up to fall down on the bed next to her.

Modern Day Adaptation~~ Okay maybe you can't adopt a snow leopard kitten, but there are options. You could substitute this for a stuffed one and get creative, a trail of rose petals is overdone. "Cum find me" written on a note is so much fun.

# Date #14 Make a Craft Together

Jenna sauntered up to him with a grin on her face, Marcus knew all too well. She was up to something. As soon as she got within arms reach of him he reached out to pull her close. She pressed her body to his and he bent to kiss her. She pressed into him but slowly started to pull back.

"What's that grin for?" He asked her.

She pushed her hips toward him and then pulled back before telling him. "I'm needy today."

His blood surged through his veins and his cock responded to her whisper. She stepped back out of his arms and told him. "I need you to help me, outside with something."

"Outside?" The cool air that flowed between them made him hesitate. They had made love outside before but it was broad daylight. He shrugged. If she wanted to make love outside in the broad light of day, who was he to tell her no? She turned away from him and headed for the front doors. He caught up to her just as she stepped outside. There in the courtyard was a long pole and the women were tying long colorful ribbons to it.

"Ah, the may pole." He pulled Jenna back to him, pressing her back to his chest and kissed her shoulder. "Everyone else will be busy with that and we can find privacy elsewhere. Good plan, m'love."

She looked up at him and shook her head. "Nope. You, my big, tough Knight are going to help raise the pole."

He turned her around to face him. "I am what?"

"You can help us raise the pole and get it set in the ground for the festivities tomorrow." Jenna batted her eyelashes at him and played innocent.

Marcus lowered his forehead to hers and growled low in his throat. "My pole is already raised, But for you alone."

She lowered her lashes and he kissed her softly. Coaxing the response he truly wanted from her. "I will do this for you, but I require a reward."

"And you'll have it." She kissed his chest where his shirt had fallen open, and walked away from him.

"Damned woman." he shook his head. He wasn't mad. How could he be? It was a simple task and would not take long. Then he would take her somewhere they could be alone, and have his way with her. If he were honest she would probably have her way with him. He grinned. He loved it when she took charge and played her way. There were things she could do he'd never dreamed of before.

So with that stupid grin plastered to his face, he followed her to the middle of the courtyard. The maypole that had been constructed was oddly shaped at the top. Instead of a rounded top. A small square box sat atop it. It seemed to be part of the pole, not an added piece. How odd. He shrugged and waited until the woman had finished tying the last ribbon on. He stepped forward and asked. "Okay, now where does this thing go?" He was jesting and Cassidy, the queen, picked up on it.

"Well, as long as you don't put it on the pile of firewood, like Hawk threatened to do, I think over here in this hole will be just fine."

"Yes, m'Lady." he smiled and let her lead the way. Just a few steps and he raised the thing over his head and set the end into the hole dug just for that purpose. "Now, I'll hold it. You ladies fill that in and pack that dirt down hard."

In a few short minutes the ladies had finished and he was able to step back to admire the work with the women all gathered round. He wrapped his arm around Jenna's waist and thought he felt a belt. He hadn't noticed a belt, but just as he was about to ask her what it was when Cassidy moved closer. "Thank you, for your help."

He let go of Jenna and bowed to his queen. " 'Tis my pleasure m' Queen."

Cassidy blushed and turned away. All these years later and she still hesitated to admit she was ruler of this land and its people.

Jenna tugged on his leather chest protector and he turned back to her. He wrapped an arm around her and led her back inside the castle.

"Where are we headed?" She whispered.

"To our chambers. I hunger for you in ways I cannot express." he bowed his head to kiss the side of hers as they walked.

Once inside, he swept them quietly past the main hall and through the dark corridors until Jenna squeezed his hand hard. She slowed her steps and pulled him back. He paused and glanced over his shoulder at her. When she pulled her hand free of his he stopped. "What is it?"

"Come here." She whispered softly. He turned to fully face her and she wrapped her arms around his neck. She pressed her lips to his and he pressed back. Gentle at first, but Jenna's hunger pushed hard at him and he would be a fool to deny her. She pushed until he walked backward into the stone wall behind him.

His arms wrapped tight around her and she pulled her lips away to gasp. "Marcus, I need you now. Please." She almost whimpered. "Marcus. Please." There was the demand. There was his woman. Her words ignited his insides and his demon roared. He growled and kissed her cheek and then her neck just above her collar bone. There he sunk his teeth deep and pulled the ever present poison from her blood. As the magic filled him, so to did his need for her. Intense and roaring through his ears, like his blood through his veins. "Jenna." He growled her name and she responded in kind. "I am yours demon."

He reached one hand between them and tore her pants from her and almost ripped his own open on the front, but at last the buttons and ties gave way. His engorged cock sprang free and Jenna glanced down between them. As her smile grew, she purred her pure satisfaction. He held the side of her face before he kissed her again and rumbled. "You like what you see, Kitten?"

"Yes, sire." She purred for him. Gods he loved that sound. He clenched his jaw tight and let her slide down the front of him. As soon as she steadied herself upon her knees she pulled his trousers away from his cock and bollocks. Cool air whispered across his manhood but just as quickly she covered it with her warm soft lips and took him deep. He put one hand on the top of her head and leaned his own against the stones behind him.

"Good girl." He growled. "That's my girl." He coaxed her as her lips moved up and down the length of him. He let her love him this way until his leg started to shake.

"Jenna. Enough." he commanded. He bent over her and lifted her under her arms. As her eyes met his, she licked her lips and smiled.

"Enjoy yourself, did ye?" He kissed her and righted himself, before dragging her down the hall to their own chambers.

As he swept her inside and bolted the door shut, her laughter finally made him hesitate. He turned around to face her and opened his mouth to ask her why she was so amused. She held the ties to her own pants as if she was the only thing holding them, because she was.

Marcus hesitated. "Why do you laugh?" He lifted an eyebrow. He was absolutely certain he was not going to like the answer.

Jenna let her pants slide down her legs and Marcus's jaw followed them. The part of her he craved most was locked behind a chastity belt like he had never seen.

"What game do you play?"

She wiggled her toes and let the trembling move up her leg. "I just wondered, I mean, I thought, You might want to fight for that which you desire." She whispered.

He pulled her into his arms, touched his forehead to hers and growled so low his chest rumbled. "Where is the key? Or would you rather I rip it off of you?"

See seemed preoccupied with the strings of his shirt. "Do you remember seeing the little wooden box on the top of the maypole?"

"I do." he said as he tilted his head to the side, waiting for the proverbial ball to drop.

"The key to what you seek is in that small wooden box." She bit her bottom lip and then ran her tongue across where her teeth had just been. His cock throbbed. He wanted her now and that damned key was outside, at the top of a damned pole.

He took her chin in his fingers and lifted her eyes to meet his. "You will suffer greatly for this, Firefly."

She wiggled her hips and grinned. "I hope so." She purred and he turned away from her. He took a deep breath and his wings burst from his back and he launched himself off the balcony. It took him all of a few seconds to reach the may pole, rip the box open and retrieve the key. With it clutched in his hand, he turned back to see Nicole hiding behind the curtains of their bed chamber window, watching him.

As his feet touched the floor of the balcony once more, he asked her. "Was that really necessary?"

"You cheated?" she stuck out her bottom lip and he pulled her close. He pressed his lips to hers and walked her back toward the bed. When the back of her knees hit the side of it, he bent her backward to lay over the bed. He finally opened his right hand and placed the tiny key in the tiny lock and was not gentle when he ripped the belt from her.

"Never, do I want to see that again." He growled and she giggled. He touched her lips with his. "Jenna. I'm serious."

"Yes, sir." She purred but the grin she tried to hide refused to go away. She was planning her next 'surprise' and he feared it would be just as this one was. His girl would always keep him on his toes.

With the belt gone, he was free to do as he pleased, but so was she. He paused and Jenna gasped.

Marcus had flipped the game. Oh no. Jenna could tell by the look on his face, she was about to be ravaged by her beast. She squirmed and wiggled and tried to pull herself up the bed away from him before he trapped her under him. Her heart pounded hard and her breath caught in her throat as his hand grabbed her hip and held her still. Damn his strength. She fought him, but not hard, because she really didn't want to get away. "Marcus." his name came out as a breathy whisper as his other hand slid underneath her to caress her. His fingers were magic and her need was building. "Marcus. I need...Marcus...I can't...Oh..." His head came down and his teeth sank into her butt cheek. "Marcus." She squealed. "Marcus, what are you..." She didn't finish her question. She couldn't. He licked that place where he had bitten and kissed and then licked As he moved over her body he continued kissing a trail up her spine to the back of her neck. His hands held her ribcage one on either side and he whispered in her ear. "Calm down. Slow your heart beat."

Easier said than done, but she took a deep breath and tried to let it out as slow as she could. She really wanted to center herself, but his fingers were now playing with her nipples and delicious sensations swept through her. She arched her back and pressed her ass into him. "Please." She whimpered. She hated when she whimpered, but right now there was no time. She needed him now. She needed his solid thickness inside her. Everything within her cried out for him. He slid one finger inside her and she whined. "More." and pushed her hips back into his hand. He nipped her shoulder and growled in her ear. "What do you want? Tell me."

"You." She whispered and licked her dry lips. "Please." The heat engulfing her body was almost too much. "Marcus."

"What part of me? Tell me what you want." He commanded and she could do nothing but obey. Her body was on fire and he was the only one who could soothe it.

"Marcus. I need you inside me. I need your cock inside me." She whispered and panted as she tried to catch her breath. She licked her lips and turned her face to look over her shoulder at him. She couldn't see him very well and she started to turn her body to look back when he barked at her. "Stay how you are."

Before she could form a thought or get words out of her mouth he raised up over her, pulled her back to the edge of the bed so her feet dangled above the floor and slid his hard cock inside her.

She sighed and let all the air whoosh out of her lungs as he pressed her deep into the mattress. His growl of satisfaction made her grin and she lifted her ass to him, urging him to move. He pressed his palm into the middle of her back. "We will do this my way."

He paused. Not moving for what felt like eternity. Then excruciatingly slowly he pulled almost all the way out. The head of his cock just at the opening of her. "Mine." He growled low and thrust into her and this time pulled back and thrust again. His strokes got harder and faster until she was certain she would pass out. She tried to take in a big breath of air just before he sped up. Stars danced in her vision and her body was on fire. "Yes, Marcus. Yes." she cried out as the sensations built higher and as the stars in her vision seemed to explode she let the release wash over her. Wrapped in the protection of his arms, Jenna finally let her body rest.

Modern Day Adaptation ~~ Okay maybe your Arts and Crafts don't have to end with a hidden key, but they could. Make something together and see where it leads or see if you work well together.

# Date # 15 Apple Picking

Keith lifted the front handles of the little cart full of apples. "I've one more bucket." Sarah hesitated. He glanced once over his shoulder and gods above help him, he could no more have said anything than he could have drawn breath at that very moment. Sarah's golden hair and pale face in the late autumn rays of the sun struck him. So was a beautiful woman, but just now, in the sun and with her hair waving freely, she was stunning.

It was as though he had never seen a woman so remarkably beautiful before in his life. He had never had the opportunity to be this close without reason before. His heart stood still. Not since his late wife had he felt these things. She stopped next to the cart and asked. "May I put one more bucket full in there before you take it back?"

He tried to clear his throat and it came out sounding more like a growl. She took a full step back and bumped into another. She turned and offered her apologies and while her back was turned he gathered himself. What in all the realms was wrong with him? He cleared his throat again and told her. "I am sorry to have startled ye', but ye are welcome to add another bucket or two if ye like. I can manage this cart easily enough."

She nodded and took a step closer. "Thank ye' sir."

Her cheeks were deep red and he wondered at it. He had not meant to be harsh in any way, but he was a bit larger than she. Mayhaps that was it. Mayhaps she was just a bit fearful. He took a deep breath and bowed to her. "Forgive my gruffness. I tend to forget myself."

"No, sir., I mean, yes, I forgive you. But there truly is nothing to forgive. I mean. It has nothing to do with you. I tend to be a bit timid." She smiled. "You have done nothing wrong, sir knight."

Keith shook his head. She started to step away and his heart tugged hard in his chest. He rubbed the center with his knuckles and called out to her. "Sarah, wait."

She stopped and looked back at him, but did not turn.

"Sarah, would you?" He set the cart of apples down carefully and went to her. He took her hands in his and asked again. "Sarah, would you join me? Walk with me while I take these apples to the courtyard?"

She simply nodded. He smiled and lifted her knuckles to his lips. He kissed them and whispered. "I would enjoy your company greatly."

Sarah couldn't keep the smile from her face. Keith was as scary and as sweet a man as she'd ever hoped to find. One who could keep her safe and provide for her. He was just a bit rough around the edges. He growled more than he talked and he seemed distant even when they had talked before. Something was missing and she hadn't yet put her finger on it. No matter what it was, that held him aloof, she had the opposite problem. She usually fell too hard and too fast and always for the wrong man. Keith was different, she reminded herself.

"I, I can't see the harm in that. I will join you." She smiled at him and tried to push down the butterflies floating in her belly. She took a deep breath and let it out slowly through her nose, so maybe he wouldn't notice.

Keith picked up the now fully loaded cart and pushed it up the trail to the inner bailey of Rogue Stone. As they walked she snatched a small apple from the pile and bit into it. Keith watched her as she chewed the bite. She smiled up at him and shrugged her shoulders. "What, I couldn't resist?"

He raised one eyebrow but made no comment. So Sarah did the thing she always did. Keith was either going to run *from* her or *into* her. "Why are you so quiet? I've seen you watching me from a distance. Do I scare you too?"

Keith threw his head back and laughed. "Scare me? Woman, you are half the size of an elf and as beautiful as a fairy." Keith stopped laughing and looked directly at her. "You do not scare me, you terrify me."

Sarah now paused her steps as he continued pushing the cart forward. So much for slowing down her heart beat. Beads of cold sweat worked their way down her spine as she tried not to choke on the last little bits of apple she'd swallowed. Was he as serious as he looked? She was terrifying? She did not think she looked so awfully bad. She had always been told she was beautiful, perhaps she had been lied to. It was possible, she supposed, for people to be dishonest. She blinked and tossed the apple core aside before she continued to follow him into the castle bailey. It was now or never. She had been bantering with Keith and hinting about things and nothing was working to get any closer to him. Something deep within her told her he was the man who could change her life, but he might also run, like all the others.

Keith, I think I have fallen in love with you, she told herself.

"Are you certain?" he asked as though nothing was out of the ordinary. Her jaw dropped when he set the cart down and turned to face her. How could he have heard the whispers of her heart?

"Do you forget, Demons can do all sorts of things humans cannot?" He smiled and she still could not make her jaw come together, lest form any sort of reply. Her breath was now coming in only short shallow burst. Before she could form words however her mind was sending all kinds of images to him and Keith took advantage. He stepped up to her and wrapped his arms around her, pinning her to his chest. He bent his head and touched his lips to hers. As he pressed she softened in his arms. He pulled back slightly to kiss her gently and then slid his tongue across her lips. Teasing and then kissing again. The second time he slid his tongue across her lips she gasped and he took his chance. He plunged his tongue inside her mouth where they tangled and danced together. He kept her trapped, until she took hold of his shirt front and wrapped her fingers in it. He brought his hands up to cover them and pulled his lips from hers. He rested his forehead on hers and said. "I'm not running, little girl."

The growl in his voice did not scare her. It made her insides quiver and her core pulse with need. Need for what, she wasn't sure. Need for him. She bent her head to hide her face in his chest. She'd never been kissed like that, but it was so good, surely it was a sin. Surely kissing a half man, half dragon, demon, was also a sin. She took a deep breath and his arms wrapped around her shoulders. "I'm keeping you." he said and kissed her again.

He kissed her neck as the words whispered through her. Her heart squeezed tight and her stomach clenched hard. Could this really be real? She took a deep breath and let the calm fill her. She leaned into Keith's embrace and let her emotions lead her.

The giggles of little girls interrupted their lovely embrace and she whipped her head around to see just who the spies were. Caden and Aurora's triplets were hiding just beyond the bushes and trying unsuccessfully to hide. She turned back to look at Keith when he suggested. "Perhaps we should take this fun in doors."

She licked her lips, looked up at him and then nodded. She was as certain about him as she was of anything in her life. There would never be another that would hold her heart. He stepped close again and took her hand in his to lead her into the darker interior of Rogue Stone. Once they were in the left side corridor, Keith pulled her behind the drapes that hung on the sides of the great hall. This was not at all private. They could be discovered at any moment.

"Do ye trust me?" Keith's whisper reached her heart and she was lost. "I can promise ye will always be mine. No matter the fates."

That was a bold promise, but one that made her heart skip a beat and the hairs on her arm stand on end. Could he make such a promise? It didn't matter. She wanted him like she had wanted nothing before in her life. Something strong pulled her to him and she would not step away. Not now. She nodded. "Yes, Keith. I trust you." As soon as the words whispered across her lips, Keith pressed her against the wall and kissed her hard. She wrapped her arms around his neck and held on as her body sang with energy. Her nipples hardened into tight buds, her insides clenched and a desperate need filled her every pore. "Please." She begged, but had no idea what for.

"I can not take ye in the hall, behind these curtains. Tis just not proper." Keith whispered between kisses.

She could not have argued if she had tried. Keith scooped her up and hurried to his chambers. The rest of the world be damned. He no more than kicked the door to his room in before he kicked his boots off and started untying the front of her dress. Her fingers fumbled with the buckles of his belt while they continued to kiss and caress each other. Sarah's face flushed hot and built until even the tips of her ears were warm. Keith kissed the tip of her right one and whispered. I care not about your past. Everything inside me tells me, ye are mine and I shall have ye. If ye say yes." He pulled back just enough to see her nod. He waited no longer to slide his pants past his hips and move her dress up and out of the way.

He took possession of her lips as she arched toward him, he slid his cock into her warm velvet core. Her cry muffled with his continued kissing. He pulled away just enough to whisper. "Stay with me, I will make you feel better than you've ever imagined." He kissed her gently as he started thrusting his hips into her. "I will show you the stars." She sunk her fingers into the hairs on his chest and wrapped her legs around him. He kissed her nose, then her cheek , then her shoulder and further still, making a trail down her arms to her finger tips. She raised her hand to him and he nibbled on her fingers as his hips kept up a maddening pace.

She tried to catch her breath but the sensations Keith was sending through her body made it hard to concentrate. She wasn't sure if she should make a noise and bit the inside of her own cheek to keep silent. Keith lowered his head and took one of her breasts into his mouth. He nipped and sucked and licked until she was mindless. All she could focus on were the sensations coursing through her and the stars floating above her. How had they gotten out of doors? Surely they were still inside Rogue Stone. "Let go." He whispered so close to her ear, her hair blew down her cheek to her neck and tickled her there. It sent warm rivers of passion coursing through her. She clenched hard around him and dug her fingernails into his shoulders as wave after wave assaulted her senses.

He slowed and his legs and stomach clenched as he roared out his release and together they lay there on his bed trying to catch their breath. She snuggled into the protection of his embrace and kissed his chest.

"You do realize, I am never letting you go." He kissed the top of her head.

"You do realize, I won't let you." She smiled up at him and sighed. Content to be right where she was for the rest of her days.

Modern Day Adaptation ~~ Obviously not much here, except perhaps you could use the apples in fun new ways, as in cooking a fun dessert to share.

# Date# 16 A Cooking Competition

The kitchen was hot when they entered. It was even hotter now, but how that was possible he wasn't sure. Megan had decided they should have a cooking competition, but just between the two of them. So on her orders Michael had left the kitchen to them with the strict warning that it would be immaculate when they returned it to him in the morning. He grinned. It would be so much fun making it messy. He knew his way around preparing a good meal. Anything that failed as a great meal he could make better with some herbs. So beating Megan in a cooking competition would be easy.

Gareth was so sure of himself. Megan scoffed. She could make a meal from almost anything. She nosed around the stores in the pantry and found some apples and spices. She would need to use caution with the nutmeg as it was a bit harder to come by, but not impossible. The cinnamon, however, she could use without worry. She got right to work and mostly ignored him, too, mostly.

Gareth was clunking through the cabinets for pots and pans and she couldn't help but laugh. He looked like such a child trying to find just what he wanted, but nothing would suit him. Were he a better cook, he would know any pot or pan will work. Megan grinned. She was already way ahead of him at this pace. She set down all her chosen goods and whispered loud enough he could hear her. "Now if only I had just the right pan." He pretended not to look up at her, but went about looking for a pan. "Hmmm." she murmured and added an "um..."

Gareth had a smile on his face that went from ear to ear as he carried a large black pan over to the stove. She shook her head and bent to take out the pan she needed. Something hit her backside. She stood up and spun on her heel to glare at Gareth....who was not even looking at her. He seemed to be busy with his tasks. Odd. She looked around on the floor and moved her skirts,but nothing was there. She was certain something had hit her in the rear end when she had been bent over.

She turned back to her work and had no sooner picked up the apple in front of her when she felt it again. Something hit her rear end. She glanced over her shoulder and still Gareth seemed to be absorbed in his work and nothing was out of place. She turned back to her work. This was no race, but she needed to get things started. She had no more than finished cutting all the apples into pieces when she felt something hit the back of her head. She spun around and this time she noticed Gareth was still doing the same thing. Just what was he doing? She moved closer and he scooped up what was in front of him and ran around the large table behind him.

"You blackard!" She gasped. "You were throwing things at me."

"Not I. I was but preparing for your attack, ma'dam." He countered and she was lost as to what to do. She turned back to her work and then turned back to him.

"My attack? Why would I do such a thing? We are to be cooking." He grinned and tossed another tiny dough ball at her.

"You scoundrel." She squealed as she ducked out of the way. She stayed down on her hands and knees and took a deep breath. Gareth hadn't played like this in such a long time. She could not keep the smile off her face. She closed her eyes for just a moment to breathe and then popped up to grab a handful of dough. Gareth threw another piece at her and missed her by mere inches. She squealed and ducked low. Her heart was pounding so hard in her chest it was all she could hear. She rolled the dough into small balls in her hand and took a deep breath before slowly raising herself up above the table to find Gareth was nowhere to be seen. Where could he have gone? From behind the pantry door Gareth jumped toward her and threw a dough ball at the same time. She squealed and ran around the far side of the table before she remembered she had a defense. She laughed out loud and turned back toward him to start pelting him with the tiny dough balls she'd made.

He threw his hands in the air and yelled. "Oh. alright. Woman ye wound me. Stop. Yow. Oh. All right now. Cease your assault on my person."

Megan kept throwing dough balls as she backed away from him until he growled and charged at her like a bear. "Ahhh." Megan squealed and backed all the way up until she hit the wall. Gareth took the opportunity to pin her there, against the wall.

Megan's breast rose and fell with her labored breathing. Gareth focused in on his prize and his tongue flicked out to lick his lips as though he would devour her in one bite. She turned her head to the side as though she were frightened. As he got closer, she raised her hands and slid her fingers up to the collar of his shirt. She curled her fingers into it, turned her face up to his and let him take possession of her lips with his own. He pressed her back until she bumped into the cabinets behind her. He took her by the waist and lifted her to sit on the top of it. He grinned as he kissed her again. Her legs wrapped around his hips at just the right height and his cock thickened.

Megan's hands slid down his shirt front and snaked their way to his belt where she made quick work of the buckle. With a couple of moves of his hips and pressing against her, he was able to rid himself of the material. His cock sprang free and he tossed her skirts out of the way. Megan gasped out loud and sucked in a big gulp of air.

He kissed her neck just beneath her ear and whispered. "Easy, Little love. Noone will come in here."

"Are you certain?" She whimpered and kissed him back.

"Very." He pulled back to move the cloth that prevented him access to his wife's treasure and slowly slid his member to the hilt. Megan threw her head back and sighed. "Yes, Gareth. Yes."

He pumped his hips and she wrapped her legs tight around him. He clenched his jaw and slowed his strokes. Until Megan was not only whimpering her velvet sheath was milking his cock. Her entire body needed release. Her entire soul needed him. He wrapped his hand around the back of her head and kissed her hard and he thrust into her. Faster, harder, harder still, not until Megan began begging did he slow.

"Tell me what you need." He growled low. "Tell me what you crave." He still held the back of her head. "Tell me."

"I need you. I need your power." She whispered and he lost control. He let go and pump thrice more when his seed burst forth and he fell over top her. He made sure to lay to the side of her, on the cabinet, their bodies still joined, panting and trying to catch his breath. He looked over to see her panting as hard as he was and brushed a loose strand of her hair from her face. She was the only one he'd ever desired like this and she would be his only until they met their end. He kissed her forehead and told her.

"I love ye, Megan."

"And I ye," Megan whispered and licked her lips.

"Ah, gods, do not tempt me so, woman." He teased her. "I'll make ye sore before we leave this room."

Megan pushed herself up off the cabinet and her whole body flushed a deep red color.

"Oh gods. I forgot where we were."

He sat up too and kissed her. "Slow your heart. We are protected." he grinned at her.

MODERN DAY ADAPTATION ~~ Clear the house if you need to, get a sitter, but try cooking together or see who is the better cook. Or try a new recipe.

# Date # 17 Rock Climbing

Jason and Lilith left the castle just before dawn and headed to the backside of the cliffs of the waterfall. Using their wings would get them to the destination, but it wasn't the destination they were after. Not really. Jason had planned an afternoon away from the castle and their duties to the king and queen. He had seen people rock climbing on his most recent trip to the future realms and it intrigued him. Lilith seemed to be interested as well, she had at least agreed to join him.

"Race ya." She shouted over the din of the horses hooves. He grinned and nodded once and they were off.

Lilith had come a long way since they had first met. He let her think she was winning this race and just as she was about to pull rein and slow her horse he let his loose.

"Whoa." Lilith pulled her foot up away from the gnashing teeth of his destrier. "Easy there. I am not the enemy." She swatted the horse and he pulled the reins back until it was under control.

"I'm sorry Lilith. I should not have used him today. I tend to forget he is also trained for battle."

She smiled. "It is all right. I will let you make it up to me."

"That, I will do." He grinned and nudged his horse forward. He navigated it through underbrush and thick stands of trees before they came to the back side of the Rogue Stone Cliffs. The area was a mess of sharp rock edges that reached into the sky with jagged narrow peaks. There were only a couple spots he and the others could even land on from above. They dismounted at the base and he waited until Lilith was standing next to him to ask. "So you think you want to climb all the way up there?"

Her smile filled her face and she looked up once again and then back at him. "Yes." She almost squealed.

"All right. If we must." He jested as though he did not want to do this, but he would do anything to spend the day with her and keep that smile on her face.

Lilith rubbed her hands together and went back to her horse's saddle. She untied the rope she had just for this purpose. "I think I brought enough. She handed him a double headed long pointed axe. He turned it over in his hands a couple of times and asked her. "What in all the realms is this?"

She put her hands on her hips. "You said you had watched others do this. Then you should know that it is a pick axe." She informed him. "It's designed to help climbers get a good hold on the rocks."

He raised one eyebrow and let his hand turn to claws.

"Okay show off." she sighed. "But if you want to do it the easy way, I guess you beat me to the top and I'll get there later. You'll just have to wait for me."

She acted like the conversation was over and stepped past him. He reached out with that same clawed hand and spun her back to him. He pinned her to his chest and bent his head to kiss her. She pressed her lips to his as her hand came up to rest on his chest, just over his pounding heart. He took her hand off his chest and brought her fingers to his lips. He kissed them and then wrapped his arm around her waist to pull her tight to him.

He pressed his lips harder and she opened to him. He sent his tongue past her teeth and into the warm welcome of her mouth where his tongue tangled with hers.

He played and let her play for a minute or so and then he pulled back to ask her. "Do you still wish to climb the hill?"

She brushed an errant piece of hair out of her face and smiled. "It is called rock climbing."

"It is called unnecessary." he quipped and when she spun around to face him he jumped back and acted as though he would pull his sword.

"Do you really need that?" She eyed the weapon where it hung from his belt.

"Usually I do, in fact, need it." he teased. "How else am I suppose to protect my girl?

"There are other ways." She turned away to continue her walk to the base of the mountain. She must really want to try this. Jason shook his head and shrugged his shoulders. Who was he to tell her no. They had nothing better to do today. He had a break from training and he could think of no better way to spend it. They would spend the time doing something not many, if any of the other warriors did. She examined the rock wall and tied a rope around her waist while he stood back and watched.

"This way, if I fall and you aren't close enough to catch me, the rope will give you more time."

"No." Jason stepped up to her and glanced at the sharp edged towering peaks. "The rope will be your hangman if you fall." he untied it from her waist and gently nudged her toward the rocks. "Go ahead and see if you can climb, I'll tend the horses, so at least they won't go missing. And I'll be right behind you."

She took a deep breath. She had never done this, but how hard could it be? As a child she had run all over her grandpa's farm and gotten into all kinds of things that she should probably wear the scars from, but luckily, she had only a couple. She glanced up again, but this time she didn't look at the top. She looked for her first hand hold. She found one and took it. She carefully placed each hand before finding footholds and repeated the process a few more times before she heard Jason call out. "You are faster than I had thought."

She turned to look down at him and he was already climbing fast to catch her. "It seems you had no trouble catching up. Are you worried I will manage to beat you to the top?" She taunted him knowing she stood no chance, but she could not lose her bravado now.

"Ah, perhaps I will wait for you, so the win is not so one-sided." He smiled and raised one hand to slowly continue to climb.

"Very funny." She stuck her tongue out at him like a child and raised one foot to push herself higher and look for the next hand hold. The only hand hold she could find was a small rock sticking out just under Jason's arm. Well, it would have to do. If she moved fast, he wouldn't even notice her. Her hand jutted over to his side and she gripped the rock and lifted her leg at the same time and tried to go faster up the rock wall. Two more grips and one more foothold and she was just above him, when she slipped.

Her heart was already pounding hard and her fingers lost their grip on the rocks in front of her. There was nothing she could do, she was falling backward.But before she could even let out a squeal. Jason's arm came around her chest like a band of steel. She hit with a loud huff. All the air whoosh out of her lungs and her heart was in her throat, making it hard to get a proper breath.

"Easy there. Go slower and you'll make it just fine." He murmured in her ear.

Wait, how was he still holding on to the wall and she couldn't keep herself on the wall? She shook her head. She didn't need to figure it out, all she needed to know was that her man had saved her and he smelled so good. She bit her bottom lip and waited until Jason set her firmly on the cliff in front of him before she turned to him to say. "Thank you. I am sorry I went too fast." She bit the inside of her cheek. She really was not sorry that she had tried to outdo him. He was so great at everything, she just wanted to have one thing she was good at here.

He turned her to face him and touched his forehead to hers. "You are good at something." He reassured her. "You make me whole."

She lowered her eyes and tried to turn from him but he held her tight. "Little girl, listen to me. You are all I need and ye need be no more than ye are."

"Jason." One word. Just his name. It was all she could manage with the lump in her throat. She swallowed and told him. "So many of you are multi-talented. I just wish to add one to my list of things I am good at."

"It doesn't need to be rock climbing. We have wings." Jason tried to reason with her, but seeing her lip quiver just before she bit it stopped him.

"Come on." He set her back on the rock face. "Let's keep going. If nothing else gets accomplished we will have exerted some pent up energy." He kissed her forehead and waited until she had a solid grip on the rocks before he completely let go.

She nodded and focused on the rock wall in front of her. It only took her another few minutes to reach the top and when she did she collapsed on the flat and threw her arms out to the sides.

"We did it." She huffed and then pulled in a breath. "We got all the way to the top without using wings."

She sat up and looked at him as he settled down next to her. "Why do people call that fun?" She asked.

He laid back to look up at the blue skies above. "One may never know." He laughed. "I have seen many odd things when I travel to the other realms with my brethren."

She rolled so she was touching him and he wrapped one arm around her to hold her close. He kissed the top of her head and she asked. "So who brought the basket and blankets up here?"

He grinned and glanced down at her. "I never doubted your abilities. I knew you would make it, but I also knew you would be thirsty if not hungry as well."

"So you took care of me." She purred and kissed his arm. "You are very sweet."

"Good gods do not tell the others." Jason teased her. "They will never let me back on the battlefield."

Lilith smiled and raised up to kiss him. She pressed a bit harder and his palm came up to rest on the back of her head, while his other hand held her to his chest. Her fingers sought his shirt and she started untying it. "Hmmm," Jason murmured. "Are you needy, m'love?"

She could not make words. She nodded and kissed him again. He wrapped both arms around her and let her keep untying his shirtfront. As it loosened she pushed it further from his chest to give her access. She kissed his exposed skin there and kept kissing until he held her tight to him and turned them over, so she lay upon the blanket. She blinked. When had he spread out the blanket?

"Magic, sugar, magic." He told her between kisses.

"Reading my mind is cheating." She responded and worked her way down to his belt. He held himself above her while she focused on releasing his manhood.

"Tis not cheating, however, ye are a greedy little minx. Who told you, you could have my cock?"

"Perhaps You haven't begged enough yet." he teased, kissed her and when she slid back up seized a nipple between his teeth.

"Ahhh." she froze. Not daring to test him. She looked up and the grin splitting his face made her giggle.

"I can wait no longer to have you." He let go of her nipple to lick her breast. First one and then the other. She ran her hands through his hair and tugged gently before she answered him.

"So take me. I am yours, demon."

He growled and his horns grew forward and she wrapped her hands around them. He shed his pants somehow and now nothing stood between them as his hard shaft touched her bare skin. She looked up into his eyes and smiled. "Do your worst, demon."

He slid his shaft into her silken velvet folds and lifted his hips until he was deep inside her. She tilted her head back and sighed. He lifted her once more and let his cock slide slowly and smoothly in and out of her. Her little moans and mews kept him hard and moving. He thrust a couple more times, with her hips in his hands and his inner demon took over. He needed more and he wanted it now. He would not be stopped. He bent his body, keeping her above him and licked her breast, first one then the other. His hands slid up her back, holding her to his chest. Her eyes fluttered open and a lazy smile pulled at her lips.

"My Demon." She sighed.

He made no words. He didn't need to. He lifted her with his hips alone and she whimpered and moaned as his hips picked up speed. She rode him hard. Her hair spilling down her back in waves and dusting his thighs. She was soft everywhere he was hard. He hugged her tight to his chest and rolled over to pin her to the blankets. This gave him better access to all of her. He rose up over her, but still covered her from the bright noon sunlight. He bent his head to kiss her and as he slid his tongue into her mouth, he slid his cock into her core. The moan he captured from her set his nerves on fire. Gods she was everything he needed and more. He thrust his hips and pulled his lips away from hers to arch his back and thrust deeper. Her hands came up to wrap around his shoulders and he lowered his head to kiss her forehead as he kept pounding. His nerves sang with energy and his blood pumped fast through his veins. He licked his lips and bent his head to her breast where he laved first one and then the other with attentions. Licking and sucking and pulling just hard enough to make her cry out and bury her fingers in the hair on his scalp.

Her body tightened beneath him and she gasped out his name. He took a deep breath and thrust one long thrust before he picked up her hips and held her while he pumped into her once, twice, three times more.

Her fingernails bit into the flesh on his arms and he grinned and pumped more. Her grip got tighter and her pants became faster. She was tossing her head from side to side and licking her lips. She was so close her sheath milked his cock from everything he could give her and He thrust just a bit faster. Anything to please his woman. He wrapped his arms around her shoulders and held her close while they both found release and she cried out his name once more.

Modern Day Adaptation ~~ Maybe try rock climbing, and maybe indoors with a trainer if you need to. Remember to keep it fun.

# Date # 18 Fly a Kite

Josephine tied the last piece of pretty lace to the tail of her kite and smiled. She had worked all day yesterday making it ready. Today Calum had promised to accompany her to the cliffs by the sea to fly her creation. She could not wait. It would look so pretty flying in the wind. She glanced up and noticed him coming toward her from across the great hall, but turned her attention back to her creation. She could not let him know he still made her warm all over. She just could not. Her cheeks felt warm but when Calum spoke the heat filled the rest of her body.

"Hello darlin'. You look lovely today." He stepped up and kissed her gently before wrapping his arms around her and pulling her to his chest. She closed her eyes and took a deep breath to pull in his scent. Her breast ached and her nipples curled into tight rosebuds and she buried her face in his chest.

His hand came up to hold the back of her head. "Why do you hide, Dear one?"

Not lifting her head from his chest she answered him. "My body betrays me every time you come near."

"Betrays you?" He whispered. "How so?"

She gasped. "Calum. I cannot tell you. Not here."

He kissed the top of her head. "Later then."

She nodded but it was all she could manage.

"Gather your kite and strings. I have the horses ready." He told her. Bless him, he did not make her elaborate on her inner thoughts. She scoffed. He was probably already reading them. She huffed and blew a piece of hair out of her face. Her hair was always coming loose from the ties. She really should find a better way to keep it out of her face. She turned back to the table and picked up the kite she had made and the string to follow Calum outside to the stables.

Indeed, two horses waited for them and each had full saddle bags. Calum stopped next to one of them and as he helped her into the saddle he said. "I thought we could have lunch while we are out on the cliffs today."

She nodded. "That is a splendid idea, it's so beautiful today and the cliffs overlooking the sea will add to that."

He nodded and mounted his horse and they were off. It took them no time at all to reach their intended destination.

"Here let me help you." Calum said as she started to dismount. He took her by the waist and picked her up off the saddle. He did not set her on her feet right away. Instead he pressed his lips to hers and let her slide down the front of his body. She stood no chance of resisting him. He smelled good and his firm chest under her fingertips pulsed with his heart beat. She closed her eyes and pictured him naked as he was last night in their bed. He kissed her again and asked. "Shall we fly this kite?"

She nodded and reached for it in her saddle bags. It took her a little more time to put it together now that she was trembling from the energy his kisses had sent through her. All she really wanted to do right now was touch him.

"Here, let me see it. I will walk toward the cliffs and see if we can get the wind to catch it." Calum suggested. "Hold tight to that string."

"Thank you." She smiled and took hold of the string to keep the kite from flying away.

Calum took the kite to the edge of the cliffs where the strong winds came up. The kite was flapping in the breeze before he even let it go. The smile that crossed Josephine's face was so worth it. He stood there like a fool watching her pull on the string and make the kite travel back and forth and to and fro in the sky above her.

"It looks like us, when we fly." She told him.

He glanced up and confirmed it. "It really does. It is not as beautiful as you though. You are far prettier."

She pulled on the kite string, making it dip and sway another time before Calum stepped up behind her wrapped his arms around her and rested his chin on her shoulder. "I love watching you play. You look so happy."

She tilted her head to the side to touch his and whispered. "I am happy, Calum. I love you and I love my life here in Hells Vein."

"Sometimes you seem far away in your thoughts." He observed and kissed her temple.

"Sometimes I am. Sometimes I let my thoughts wander and I'm back in the past reliving the nightmares, but the more memories we make like this one, the more good times I will have to look back on."

"I love ye, Josephine." He turned her around in his arms and she let the kite glide to the ground as he pressed his lips to hers once again. He pulled back, took her hand and led her to the horses. He let go of her hand to retrieve a blanket from the saddlebags and then took up her hand again. He kept silent until they reached a copse of trees and he had the blanket laid out.

"Come here." He murmured and she lowered herself to his lap. He wrapped his arms tight around her and they watched the birds floating on the breeze like her kite had done just moments before. She turned her head and he leaned forward to connect with an awkward kiss. They both laughed and she took a deep breath and gathered her courage. She turned around and straddled his legs to face him.

"Ah, it is a much better view now." Calum smiled.

"Is it now?" She asked as her cheeks filled with heat. Would her shyness ever go away?

Calum answered her silent question. "I hope it never does. I like that quality about you."

She kissed him and he kissed her back, his tongue probed for entrance and she granted it. Their tongues danced and paired and slid in and out of each other, like promises of things to come. Calum took her by the waist and set her aside. "I must have you." He kissed her and started to untie her dress front.

She could not respond. She was doing all she could to catch her breath, which did not help her case at all. Her breasts were rising and falling quickly, keeping Calum's attention. It was not long and their clothes were discarded in a heap at the edge of the blankets.

"Gods I am a lucky man." Calum breathed the words next to her ear as his hands slid up her back and pulled her close to him. He kissed her neck, nipped her earlobe and licked a trail down her jawline back to her lips. She could not hide her reaction from him now, and his hands found her breasts and he rolled a nipple between a thumb and finger. Tingling sensations coursed through her and she gasped.

"That's it, feel those sparks." Calum whispered and slid one hand down between them to caress her secret folds and one finger eased inside her.

She bit her lip and nodded because words were impossible with the energy coursing through her. Everything was on fire. Everything was so hot but oh so good. She rubbed herself on his hand. Begging him for more. She could no longer hold back and whimpered his name.

"Easy, love. I've got you." He whispered and nipped her earlobe again.

"Please." She could not stop herself. It was just so good. She rocked her hips forward and he slid another finger inside her. His other arm held her to him as he laid her down on the blankets. Josephine concentrated on the clear blue sky above until Calum's lips took hold of her nipple. She brought her hands to his head and ran her fingers through his hair, and tugged at the short dark strands at the nape of his neck. She trailed her toes up the back of his leg as she held onto his shoulders tighter now as euphoria built higher and higher inside her.

He laved her nipples with attention, one after the other and finally he raised up over her, kissed the tip of her nose, and held himself above her. When her eyes finally met his, she gasped as the tip of his manhood slid deep inside her core. He filled her to the hilt and started slow rhythmic strokes. She raked her nails down his chest as he thrust slowly in and pulled slowly back out.

Their lips met in a slow gentle caress, until Calum lifted his hips high enough, he was just barely inside her. He held for a moment before he shoved his hips forward. Her back rubbed against the blankets and suddenly she was grateful they had them. Thrust after thrust she held onto him and suddenly she could not get enough of him. She needed more. She needed deeper. Harder. Faster. "Please." She panted the words. Too caught up in the passion to breathe properly. She huffed. "Calum. I need. Ah…" She could not finish her sentence. She raised her hands to her head and ran her fingers through her own hair to hold her head. It was spinning so fast now. Stars exploded behind her eyes and she cried out to him. "Calum." His name a breathless plea. "Now."

Calum picked up his pace and obeyed her pleas. He could not do anything other than please her. His demon would not let him. He thrust once more and kissed her as her release and his hit at the same moment. He swallowed her cry and added his own growl.

He wrapped her in his arms and laid down beside her to let the breeze off the cliffs cool their heated bodies.

Modern Day Adaptation~~ Go fly a kite anywhere you pick. The park, the beach, a pasture. Just make sure you are safely away from others before you add the naughty parts.

# Date # 19 Breakfast in Bed

Lucas stretched his body out on the bed pulling the blankets down his chest and revealing the top of Raven's head. She slept soundly next to him. A glance to his right revealed no light coming from between the curtains either. It was still early enough he might be able to slip out unseen by most everyone. Now, if he could just get out from underneath his lovely wife. He pulled himself upright and she snuggled into his side. Now he could snug the blankets in next to her as though he was still by her side and slip away unnoticed.

He pulled on a pair of pants, forgoing his boots, and made his way down the corridor to the kitchens. Micheal was already there preparing the morning meal, as Lucas suspected he would be.

"Ah, what brings ye to the kitchens so early?" Micheal asked.

"I'd like to give Raven time to rest today. So I thought we might watch the sunrise from our bed."

"Ah bedsport will make a lad hungry." Micheal teased."Here take some cheese and some bread. I have apples and a wee bit o' honey too."

Lucas and Micheal gathered all the things and just before Lucas scooped up the tray, Micheal handed him a pitcher. "Do not forget the drinks."

Lucas nodded and hurried back to his chambers. He wanted to make sure he was back before the sun rose and so did his mate.

He glided across the floor and leapt up the stairs to arrive at his bedchamber door. Slowly, ever so carefully he opened it and slid inside. He paused for a moment to make sure Raven still slept soundly and then made his way to the balcony. There he set the tray of food and pitcher of mead. He tossed a couple of pillows on the settee and picked it up to set it at the entrance of the balcony. There they could watch the sun rise and as it rose so would they. He shed his clothes and slipped back into bed next to his mate.

He kissed the side of her head and nipped at her ear and kissed her shoulder. Her eyelashes fluttered and she softly moaned his name. His cock was instantly at attention. She leaned back against him and pressed her ass into his groin and he kissed her cheek.

"Needy are we?" He whispered in her ear and nibbled at her lobe. She smiled and raised her shoulder to try fending him off.

"If you want me to stop you'll have to try harder than that, sugar." he challenged her.

"Hmmm." she moaned and stretched out next to him. "It's too early for challenges."

"Ah, but not to see the sun rise." He kissed her full on the lips when she finally turned back to him.

"Lucas. I've always wanted to see a sunrise here in Rogue Stone." Her eyes popped open and she moved to sit up. He put one hand on her chest and pushed her back down.

She blinked and he leaned over her to kiss her. "You have time. First my cock needs some attention."

She grinned. "Hmm...but I'm so tired." She yawned.

"A bore am I?" He teased and tossed back the covers. The cool air from the room breezed across Raven's bare skin and made her nipples perk to two tiny peaks. He leaned over her and took one in his mouth to lick and nip and suck until she cried out.

"Cease and I will follow you to the ends of the earth, beast." He let go of her nipple and grinned.

"You already have, sugar. 'Tis no real promise now. Ye'll have to do better than that."

She ran her fingers through his hair and arched her back toward him. While he was caught up watching her breasts, she snaked a hand down between them and took hold of his rather large member.

His hissed breath told her all she needed to know. He was the one now captured and she was the one now in control. She scooted herself down the bed to bring her lips to his cock and she kissed him there. Then a slow lick up his length, then down again, to cup his ballocks with her soft palm.

"Enough woman. You wanted to see the sun rise." He sat up and pulled her up with him. "If we continue, you will miss it."

He picked her up off the bed and took her to the settee on the balcony. Nearby was a small table with a tray of fruits and bread and cheeses'. She smiled and kissed his chest where he held her.

"Lucas. Thank you." She told him. "This is lovely."

He kissed her forehead and set her on the soft cushions. "Then sit here with me, and watch it rise."

"The sun?" She asked playfully?

"Or what ever else ye desire." He grinned and stroked himself while standing in front of her. Her cheeks turned red and she glanced at her lap.

He held out a cup of mead to her and told her. "Here. Take this."

She obeyed but still would not look at him.

"What has you blushing?" He wondered out loud.

"Look to my thoughts. I can not bring myself to say the words out loud."

'*Ah, I see now.*' He sent her love and comfort as he kissed her temple. '*There is no need to be nervous. Noone else is awake and no one else will be looking up at our balcony.*'

'*I know.*' She sent him and rested her head on his shoulder.

He wrapped an arm around her shoulders and pulled her tight to him for a moment. She took a sip of her mead and leaned forward to set it aside. As she brought her hand back she brushed the head of his cock with her fingers. He flinched and she giggled. He was so easy. Every nerve in her was on fire and her whole body was coiled tightly, waiting for what he would do next.

He took hold of her chin, lifted it so their eyes met and kissed her. Gentle at first, then his hand palmed the back of her head and she was caught. She wrapped her arms around his neck as the sky lightened and dark clouds turned a dusky purple with hints of pink. He pulled away and took hold of her waist. She blinked at him and then looked down at his hands where they wrapped around her waist. Without any effort, he picked her up and sat her on his lap to face the sunrise. His cock rested on her back, the base nestled perfectly between her cheeks. The fire that coursed through her at the thought of his need of her was vicious and all consuming.

"Lucas." Was all she could manage.

He leaned forward, brushed her long hair over her shoulder to cover her breast and whispered. "What do you want, sugar? Tell me," he rubbed her back, slowly, up and down, then curled his fingers and used his knuckles to add pressure. She leaned into the warmth of his strong hands.

"Lucas, I need." She moaned and fanned her face with her hand. "I want you."

"Look up." he whispered and lifted her up.

She looked up and as he slid her down on his velvet steel shaft, the clouds drifted apart and let the sun start to rise on the horizon. The yellows and pinks and purples of the morning sunrise were as breathtaking as his length filling her.

"Lucas." His name whispered across her soft lips was all he needed. He raised his hips and gave Raven the ride she craved. Thrusting and lowering until she was bouncing on his lap. He reached around and took her breast in his palms then to pinch and twirl her nipple in his fingers made her cry out.

"Tell me what you need." He pulled her back to his chest and wrapped his palm around her exposed throat. "Tell me what your body craves."

"You. I need you. Harder. Please. More please." Raven wasn't sure what she was asking for. It was already so much. Could it be as she asked for? How could...her thoughts vanished when Lucas squeezed her breast hard, then let go to hold her hips as he thrust harder into her, almost throwing her to the floor. She grabbed onto his knees to keep herself from hitting the floor as he pumped into her. Thrust after thrust sent molten lava coursing through her so hot she was gasping for air by the time he slowed his strokes.

"Come with me." She didn't think she was close but as he said those words euphoria swept her up and as the sun burst forth with its bright rays, stars burst behind her eyes.

"Lucas." She cried out as he grunted one last time and wrapped her in his arms to pull her back to his chest.

"Gods you are too good for me." He whispered and kissed the side of her neck. She rested her head on his shoulder and let the early morning sun bathe them in light.

Modern Day Adaptation~~ Not much needed here. A bedroom, some careful planning and maybe your breakfast will be forgotten too.

# Date #20 Trivia Night in a Bar (NSFW- use Caution.)

Everyone had gathered in the great hall. Elites', Protectors, and workmen and women all. Nicole took another look around the hall to make certain no children or young ones were present. She leaned back against Dalton and he kissed the top of her head.

"I think now." She told him out loud.

*'It is for you to decide, love.'* He communicated to her.

She smiled and made eye contact with Cassidy and she blushed before she turned away. Nicole had already asked and was granted permission by her queen. She had never attempted anything like this before in her life, but she trusted everyone of the Elite's to keep her safe.

Nicole stood up and went to the front of the room near the fireplace. She took a deep breath, made eye contact with Dalton and clapped her hands a couple times until everyone was looking at her.

"Thank you for your attention." She cleared her throat. "I wanted to teach you a new game."

The warriors cheered.

"Unmated Elite's, you need to all be at one table. Mated Elite's to the other." She waited until everyone had changed seats. "Now the same for the Protectors and all the others."

"Now. There will be a series of questions about each other and the things that have happened here in Rogue Stone. The group that answers the most questions correctly wins." Nicole explained. "Where I come from they call it Trivia. You might understand it better if we call it trivial information." She laughed at the odd looks she was getting.

"It involves drinking and mates." She whispered the last word, because as much as this might be her ultimate fantasy, she was still nervous she would step wrong. Warriors never shared their mates. It was absolutely unheard of.

"And your prize for winning this game," She paused with her heart hammering in her chest and her throat dry as the arizona rocks, until each warrior was looking at her. "Will be me and any other you choose."

She expected a roar but the quiet that followed and the looks Dalton got from his brethren she had not expected. Not really.

"Nicole." Hawk stood up. "Nicole has already asked permission for this and none of you must play the game. It is your choice."

The group looked around the room in disbelief, and then at Dalton. "You allow this? She is yours. Ye'll not gut us like fish?"

Dalton shook his head. "Nay, friends. This is how she likes to play. The play means nothing. My heart is hers and hers is mine. The play is strictly that. Play. We are Eternal Mates, taking it further is impossible."

"So be it." One stated.

Then another. "I'm in."

Nicole smiled.

"Hey, wait." Gareth called out above the murmurs of the others. "What if the mated group wins the game?"

Nicole smiled. She wondered how long it would take him to recall that little fact. "Then you get to make the call. We can either stay here in the hall and everyone enjoy and partake of whomever, however, they would like, or ye can separate to your own privacy."

"Is everyone clear?" Hawk asked. "Is everyone comfortable?"

Cheer's rent the air and Nicole sauntered back over to Dalton to press a kiss to his lips. He pulled her onto his lap and kissed her hard. The men cheered and toasted to him and Nicole and finally he tossed her up on her feet so she could start the game.

"Do we really need a game?" Someone asked.

"Aye. Let us get warmed up first." Another answered.

Nicole clapped her hands again and all of them looked up at her.

"So first question. Who among us was the first to figure out the blood bond?"

Some shouted "Hawk." others "Cassidy."

"The Mates table got that one." Nicole shouted over the din.

Boo's came from the Unmated table and she smiled. "Step up your game boys."

"Who are ye callin' boys?" Caden asked.

Nicole didn't answer. She simply raised an eyebrow.

"Next question." She waited until they quieted. "Who was the one who saved Hawk in the battle last summer?"

The men whispered among themselves and finally the Unmated group shouted, "It was Caden."

"Aye, but then it was I who healed him." Cassidy herself shouted.

"Ah, but the question was who saved him." Nicole corrected.

"So one point for the unmated group."

And so it went until both teams had stacked a bunch of points. It was anyone's game and Nicole's heart was racing. She licked her lips before asking the last question. She knew who would get this one and she knew the outcome. She had dreamed of this all her life.

She cleared her throat. "If you could stop kissing and fondly your mates and potential mates for a moment, I'll ask the last question."

Gareth and Hawk both glanced up at her with stupid grins on their faces. "Go ahead."

She nodded and licked her lips. "Who carried Cassidy into the tunnel the night of the massacre at Lounsbury Castle?"

A hush fell over the group and just about the time the men started to growl about someone better have the answer.

Calum stood up and Cassidy's jaw dropped. Nicole glanced back at her queen and there were tears in her eyes.

"It was I." Calum's voice didn't waver.

"That's another point for us." Lucas shouted and the unmated Elites and other warriors cheered.

Nicole stepped up to Dalton who had already started to come toward her. "Thank you, Sir."

He touched his forehead to hers and silently replied. *'Do not think you will be the only one to enjoy this.'*

She pressed her lips to his and let her instincts guide her. A moment later he pulled back and nodded to someone behind her. He started to unbutton her shirt and from behind her someone took hold of her hips. Then he leaned his head low to kiss her neck and then lick her ear. She closed her eyes and purred. He grabbed a handful of her long dark hair and pulled her head back exposing her throat. Dalton grinned and took the offering. He lowered his lips to her neck and kissed and licked her there before sinking his fangs deep. Magic exploded inside her and every nerve stood at attention. He wrapped his arms around her, pulling her tight to his chest. Damn this was good. All the sensations at once. She opened her eyes just briefly to glance around the room. Some couples had indeed stayed. Nicole reached her hand back to touch the side of Keith's head and ran her fingers through his hair. She arched back toward him, pushing her breasts toward Dalton.

Keith's hands on her hips pulled her back toward him and she let herself be pulled away from Dalton. He had pulled the poison from her and just now she was alive with the energy coursing through her. She leaned forward and kissed Keith and Rance took Dalton's place. Ah the more exotic one. Rance had always caught her attention with his golden eyes that followed her like a jungle cat. The men massaged and rubbed her all over. One reached to cup her breast in the warmth of his palm while another suggested they move her to the settee and set her on top of his large frame. Her cheeks heated and Dalton sent her *'Are you certain? Your heart races with your eyes closed.'*

*'Yes, Sir.'* She paused for a moment to lick her lips and sent him. *'Thank you, Sir.'*

She glanced up in time to see Dalton kissing another woman, she did not care who, as she was being lowered on top of Rance. He was already hard and pulsing for her. She licked her lips as her eyes met his and asked. "You want me?" She was stunned. She was protected in this group, but never had she guessed she was wanted.

"How could I refuse, such a goddess, if this is what she desires?" He countered and she was at a loss for rebuttal. She moaned as his shaft filled her and his hands wrapped around her waist holding her firm until she had adjusted. Just as her eyes fluttered open, Dalton's voice reached her. "I love seeing my woman worshiped."

Rance lifted her using only his hips and the ride began. He was thrusting and tossing her up and forward. She leaned into his chest and held on to his arms as best she could as his hard shaft slid in and out of her heat over and over again. Rough calloused hands came from behind her to hold and caress her breast. He rolled first one nipple and then the other between his thumb and finger. He bent his head to murmur "Good girl." Her skin erupted in goosebumps followed close by a wave of fire that sent every nerve dancing. Stars danced behind her half closed eyelids and her heart raced. Her blood surged through her veins as energy like she'd never felt before coursed through her and she gasped.

"Ah. There it is." Rance commented. "Now open those beautiful eyes."

Another warrior picked her up under her arms and lifted her off of Rance's shaft. She whimpered and stuck her bottom lip out in a childish pout.

"Now now, we can't have you getting a release already. None of us has had that yet and neither shall you." He told her. She glanced at Dalton but found no help there either. Truth be told, she didn't want any. The delicious sensations sweeping through her were so much better than she had ever imagined.

Another man was brought before her and she lowered herself to her knees, took his cock in her hand and licked up the length of him. Then back down to take him fully into her warm wet mouth. His groan was all the encouragement she needed. The murmurs and grunts from the others were just a bonus. She pulled back and grinned up at him. She had this man literally in the palm of her hand and he would do anything she asked. Power swept through her and she glanced at Dalton once more.

"This needs to happen more often." She purred.

The men present cheered and one of them lifted her up to stand facing Keith. She leaned back to see who her next suitor might be and was not surprised to see Calum. He leaned low to whisper. "Now let us see how you handle two warriors."

Her body flushed with heat. Was this really going to happen? Her wildest dreams were coming true? She smiled at Dalton and could not wipe the smile from her face until Calum's cock slid into her warm wet sheath, only to glide back out and probe at her rear. She took a deep breath and braced herself against Keith's wide chest. He leaned down and held the back of her head in his hand when he whispered.

"If you relax it will go easier."

Easier said than done, when she was so excited to finally be able to play. Keith played with her breast. Fondling and caressing and sucking. Calum tried again and again, she was too tense. Suddenly Keith was gone and Dalton was there pressing his lips to hers and as she relaxed into him, Calum slid his cock into her. Way in to her. She gasped against Dalton's lips and he smiled.

"That's my girl." Now take a deep breath and relax so Keith can share you."

She could only nod as Calum was sliding his cock slowly in and out of her rear. Every nerve was snapping and energy surged through her. This. Yes. This. All she could manage for a reply was to whimper. "Uh huh."

Dalton kissed her again on the top of her head and tugged her hair before retreating once more to another.

Keith's chest blocked her view, but she didn't care. Keith kissed her cheek, then her chin, never her lips. Then as gently and as slowly as Calum had entered her rear, Keith slid his shaft into her warm velvet heat. She sighed and whispered against his chest. "Fuck, yes. Thank you sir."

Keith chuckled and started pumping hard against her and Calum returned the thrust from his side. Keith pressed deeper and his second thrust had his balls slapping her in turn with Calum's from behind. She gasped and another warrior took hold of her chin. She glanced up and then down at his cock. He held himself level with her lips. She licked them and grinned. He waited for her to take the lead. She wrapped her fingers around his cock and licked and sucked until she wasn't sure if it was her moaning or him.

Her head spun and there was no doubt it was she who was moaning. "Dalton, please."

"Ah she calls for her mate." One man taunted. "He can not help ye now. Ye belong to us."

Her heart pounded and she gasped as another man took Calum's place and he came to her side to whisper his thanks. "You were such a good girl," he whispered. "I think it is time you had your reward."

She could only nod as she slid her lips up and down the length of the man in front of her and Keith's cock moved faster within her. His own release coming hard and fast.

"Uh-huh." She mumbled and licked her lips before sliding them back over the cock. "Thank you, sir." She whimpered when he pulled on her hair to pull her head up to him. Just before his lips touched hers. Dalton.

"That is a line ye'll not cross, brother." The warning he gave Calum seemed to shake the other man out of whatever trance he was in because Calum backed away quickly nodding to Dalton.

Dalton blocked her view of the retreat and whispered in the tone she could not resist. "Come for me."

Keith lifted her off his cock just and Dalton turned her to lean over the settee. In this position she could take Keith's cock into her mouth as Dalton filled her. With her mate filling her she did not need two to make the euphoria explode inside her.

"Dalton. Now. Please." She panted and prayed he would not hold back.

The first thrust of his hips almost made her bite Keith. She pulled his cock from her mouth to lick her lips and compose herself for the barest of moments before taking him back into her mouth. Dalton increased his pace and she was barely able to keep up.

Unable to bear more, she slid her lips up Keith's shaft once more as Dalton thrusted; she could only slide her fingers up and down Keith's hard shaft. He grunted and she grinned. One glance at his eyes and they connected. She opened her mouth to take him as he found release and stars exploded behind her closed eyes as well, when Dalton grunted. "Good Girl."

She collapsed against Keith's chest and Dalton pulled away. She had no more than caught her breath when Dalton picked her up and carried her away. She could only assume it was to their chambers for some much needed cuddling. She sighed and he kissed her forehead.

"I love you."

"I love you too." He whispered.

MODERN DAY ADAPTATION ~~ Well, no need to adapt, unless you need to find the right group, or club. Maybe just stick with trivia in a bar and a fun night afterward. Your comfort level is the most important factor here.

Did you love *Date Nights in Rogue Stone*? Then you should read *Warriors Secret*[1] by McKayla Jade!

A massacre the likes of which not many have witnessed, leaves Cassidy at the mercy of her distant and greedy uncle. Every step forward proves the world she once knew has disappeared. Lost in an unfamiliar world of strict rules and harsh punishments, Cassidy's last hope may be a baron she's quickly falling in love with, but that comes with a price.

Lord Ian Hawkins never believed he would meet a woman who could ride beside him in battle, much less one who would stir his heart. He should let her go. HIs world is full of secrets

---

1. https://books2read.com/u/bQN8Yv

2. https://books2read.com/u/bQN8Yv

and shadows. He would go to the ends of the earth for her but he would never ask her to follow.

Read more at https://www.authormckaylajade.com/.

# Also by McKayla Jade

**Elite Warrior Novel**
Warriors Secret
Warriors Trust
Warriors Worth
Warriors Honor
Warriors Vengeance


**Rogue Stone After Dark**
Date Nights In Rogue Stone
Date Nights in Rogue Stone


Watch for more at https://www.authormckaylajade.com/.

www.ingramcontent.com/pod-product-compliance
Lightning Source LLC
Chambersburg PA
CBHW051253160726